Rosa's Big Boat Experiment

Yap!
Yap!

Child's Play (International) Ltd
Ashworth Rd, Bridgemead, Swindon SN5 7YD, UK
Swindon   Auburn ME   Sydney
ISBN 978-1-78628-363-4   WP281119CBB03203634
© 2020 Child's Play (International) Ltd
Printed in Guangdong, China
1 3 5 7 9 10 8 6 4 2
www.childs-play.com

Rosa and her friends are getting
ready to build some boats.
"How many cups will it take to fill
our tray?" asks Sadiq.

"The boats will need to float," says Jamil.
"What about this log?" asks Lottie.
"That's much too big," replies Jamil.
"It will sink!"

"Amazing!" says Jamil. "It DOES float!"
"The wood floats because it's less
dense than the water," explains Rosa.

"Everything is made of molecules," says Lottie. "They are very, very tiny. The closer the molecules are packed together, the denser the object."

"Let's see," predicts Jamil. "This ping-pong ball should float because it's less dense than water."

"This marble is the same size as the ping-pong ball," says Sadiq. "Why doesn't it float too?"

Lottie is experimenting.
"If you put something heavy in the water, the water level rises," she notes.
"That's called displacement," says Jamil.

They go outdoors.
"Out here there's lots more water,"
says Rosa. "We can test which
things will make the best boats."
"Can I go first?" asks Sadiq.

"Oh no! My sponge has absorbed water," says Sadiq. "It's too heavy and it's sunk! What can I use now?"

"Do boats fill up with water when it rains?" laughs Lottie. "Mine's sinking!" "We could have a boat race!" says Rosa.

"Which shape of boat do you think will go the fastest?" asks Jamil. "A pointed shape at the front cuts easily through the water," says Rosa.

Wheee!

"I'm going to add a sail," says Rosa.
"The wind will blow into the sail
and make the boat go faster."

"I'm making a sail too!" exclaims Sadiq.
"My boat's going to be the fastest!"
"I've made the hull pointed at the front!"
says Lottie.

"All our boats float really well," says Rosa. "Now we'll know what to use next time!"